THE PROUD AND
FEARLESS LION

For Molly Franklin

A Red Fox Book

Published by Arrow Books Limited
20 Vauxhall Bridge Road, London SW1V 2SA
An imprint of The Random Century Group

London Melbourne Sydney Auckland
Johannesburg and agencies throughout the world

First published by Hutchinson Children's Books 1986

Beaver edition 1988

Reprinted 1989 (twice)

Red Fox edition 1990

Set in Worcester Round by Citype Ltd,
4 West Walk, Leicester LE1 7NB

Printed and bound in Great Britain
by Scotprint, Musselburgh, Scotland

ISBN 0 09 955470 4

THE PROUD AND FEARLESS LION

Ann & Reg Cartwright

RED FOX

ONCE THERE WAS A PROUD AND FEARLESS LION.
Every morning at the same time he
would go into the jungle and roar his
mighty roar. So terrifying was this
roar that all the animals would run away and
hide; and so loud was this roar that the ground
would shake and the leaves would fall from
the trees.

'That'll show 'em who's boss!' said the proud
and fearless lion.

One night word went round the jungle that it
would rain. 'There will be a great storm,' said the
little mouse. 'We must all take shelter.'

The big animals sheltered in a cave, the smaller
ones in holes in the ground, and the birds
snuggled together in the trees.

'Pooh!' said the proud and fearless lion. 'A little
rain never hurt anyone.' And just to show how
proud and fearless he was, he climbed to the top
of his favourite hill and went to sleep. All night
long it rained and rained, but on he slept.

The next morning the rain had stopped and the jungle was unusually quiet. A gentle mist hung over the trees and everywhere was still. Mouse woke up, sniffed the air and listened for Lion's roar. But for the first time ever it did not come.

That's strange, thought Mouse.

One by one the animals emerged, and because
there was no sign of Lion they were not afraid.
Hippo decided to take a bath, but Mouse was
curious to discover what had happened to Lion.

'I think we should go and search for him,'
she squeaked.

'Whatever for?' grumbled Giraffe. 'He's always
been a show-off, roaring and frightening us.'

'I know he makes a lot of noise,' said Mouse.
'But has he ever hurt you?'

The animals had to agree that Lion had
never hurt anyone.

So the animals set off to look for Lion. They found him on top of his hill. He opened his mouth to roar, but only a little squeak came out, followed by ATISHOO! He was no longer a proud and fearless lion – just a soggy, saggy, snivelling lion with drooping whiskers.

'You don't look so frightening now,' said Mouse bravely. 'I think you have a bad attack of soricus throaticus. It's brought on by too much roaring and sleeping in the rain. We can cure you with honey and Eucalyptus leaves, but if we make you better you must promise not to frighten us again.'

Lion tried to say, 'I promise,' but he could only squeak and nod his head.

Mouse sent the bees off to search for
nectar to make into honey, and the animals
and birds collected the Eucalyptus leaves.
For two whole days they nursed and comforted
Lion; and for two whole nights he slept and
dreamed and sneezed and coughed. By the third
morning he began to feel better.

The proud and fearless lion stood up and
stretched his legs. 'Good morning, animals,' he
said politely. But there was no reply. He walked
down his hill and into the jungle calling, 'Tiger!
Hippo! Giraffe! Little Mouse! Is anybody there?'

But the jungle was as sad and silent as if the
animals had never existed.

Lion searched through the jungle for many miles.
All of a sudden, the little mouse came scurrying
towards him.

'Oh, brave Lion,' she cried. 'Come quickly.
While you were sleeping two hunters came and
drove the animals into a cage. They are being
taken away from the jungle to join a circus.
Because I am so small, I managed to escape
through the bars.'

When Lion heard Mouse's story he began to feel
his pride and fearlessness coming back. The
jungle would not be the jungle without the
animals. 'Climb on to my head, little one,' he said.
'We must go and find them.'

Mouse knew a short cut and Lion followed her
directions through the deepest, darkest part of the
jungle, where no flowers grew and only snakes
lived under the tangled leaves.

On and on they went until they came to the very edge of the jungle. In the moonlight Lion and Mouse could see two hunters sitting by a camp fire. The poor animals were locked in a cage. It was a terrible sight! Elephant's trunk was all squashed up and Giraffe's neck was stuck between the bars.

That night Lion and Mouse lay down together and fell asleep trying to think of a plan to save the animals.

By the time the sun had risen over the jungle the next morning, they had a plan. Mouse sat on top of Lion's head so that only she could be seen over the top of the bush. 'Now squeak, Mouse,' whispered Lion. And Mouse squeaked as loudly as she could until the hunters heard her.

'That's the mouse who escaped!' shouted one hunter.

'After her!' called the other.

But that was their biggest mistake. . . .

Lion leaped out from behind the bush, roaring the loudest and most terrifying roar he had ever roared. ROARRRRRRR! It echoed through the jungle, and the earth shook and the leaves fell from the trees.

'That'll show 'em!' said the proud and fearless lion.

The terrified hunters fell over, dropping their guns and the keys to the cage. Mouse picked up the keys and ran to free the animals.

Soon all the animals were out of the cage, 'Thank you, proud and fearless lion,' they said.

'No trouble,' Lion replied. 'Now let's teach those hunters a lesson!'

So they all lined up, the smallest on the left and the biggest on the right.

'Charge!' shouted Mouse. And the animals roared and chattered and squawked and screeched and they chased the hunters out of the jungle for ever.

As they trooped back home, Lion realized he had never felt quite so proud and fearless before. And he kept his promise never to frighten the animals again.

But if those hunters ever came back. . . well, that would be another story!

Other Titles in the Red Fox picture book series (also incorporating Beaver Books)